SARAH RISING

by
TY CHAPMAN

illustrated by
DeANN WILEY

beaming books

MINNEAPOLIS

Text copyright © 2022 Ty Chapman
Illustrations copyright © 2022 DeAnn Wiley

Published in 2022 by Beaming Books, an imprint of 1517 Media.
Printed in the United States of America.

28 27 26 25 24 23 22   1 2 3 4 5 6 7 8 9

Library of Congress Cataloging-in-Publication Data

Names: Chapman, Ty, author. | Wiley, DeAnn, illustrator.
Title: Sarah rising / by Ty Chapman ; illustrated by DeAnn Wiley.
Description: Minneapolis, MN : Beaming Books, an imprint of 1517 Media,
   2022. | Includes bibliographical references. | Audience: Ages 5-8. |
   Summary: Inspired by the Minneapolis uprising after the killing of
   George Floyd, this story follows a little Black girl attending a protest
   with her father and realizing that she has the power to protect what and
   whom she loves. Includes author's note.
Identifiers: LCCN 2021028764 (print) | LCCN 2021028765 (ebook) | ISBN
   9781506478357 (hardcover) | ISBN 9781506478364 (ebook)
Subjects: LCSH: Protest movements–Juvenile fiction. | Fathers and
   daughters–Juvenile fiction. | Missing children–Juvenile fiction. |
   African American girls–Juvenile fiction. | CYAC: Protest
   movements–Fiction. | Fathers and daughters–Fiction. | Lost
   children–Fiction. | African Americans–Fiction. | LCGFT: Picture books.
Classification: LCC PZ7.1.C4847 Sar 2022 (print) | LCC PZ7.1.C4847
   (ebook) | DDC 813.6 [E]–dc23
LC record available at https://lccn.loc.gov/2021028764
LC ebook record available at https://lccn.loc.gov/2021028765

Hardcover ISBN: 978-1-5064-7835-7
eBook ISBN: 978-1-5064-7836-4

VN0004589; 9781506478357; MAY2022

Beaming Books
PO Box 1209
Minneapolis, MN 55440 -1209a
Beamingbooks.com

For Philando Castile, Jamar Clark, George Floyd, Winston Smith,
their families, and Black people everywhere.
—T.C.

For Mama Rachelle, Mama Candy, Jasmine, Raquel,
Genesis, Trevon, Destiny, and Bailey.
—D.W.

My morning started like any other.
I ate most of my toast before running
out the door to find food for my pets.

Once I found enough leaves,
I fed them to my beetles, and I
put some toothpaste in my ant farm.
They like it! Don't tell my dad.

With everyone fed, I started getting ready for school.

But then, Dad came into my room.
He said I wasn't going to school today.
"Sarah, we're going to a protest."

Dad told me that the police had killed another Black person. "They're supposed to serve and protect us," he said, "but they hurt us instead.

"That's why we have to keep each other safe and stand up for what's right."

Soon we saw a huge crowd of people. They were all shouting for justice. I grabbed Dad's hand, and we walked into the crowd.

It was loud and scary, but I knew I was safe with Dad. He held my hand tight and began yelling with the crowd, "No justice, no peace!"

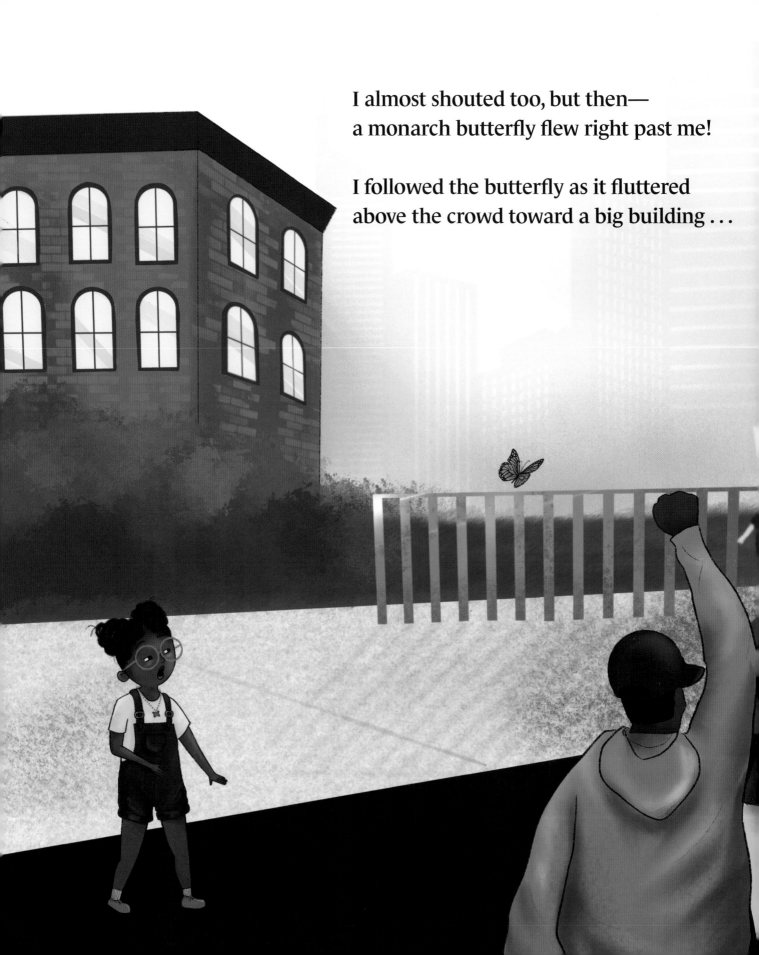

I almost shouted too, but then—
a monarch butterfly flew right past me!

I followed the butterfly as it fluttered
above the crowd toward a big building . . .

. . . until it flew right in front of a cop's face.

He jumped back, like he was stung by a wasp.
He smacked the colorful monarch out of the air.
It fell to the ground and didn't get back up.

I knew I had to do something. We have to keep each other safe and stand up for what's right. I ran toward the butterfly.

The cop started shouting. "GET BACK!" he roared. He looked at me like I had done something wrong.

I ran back into the crowd, pushing past people as tall as trees.
A cop's job is to protect us, so why do they hurt us, instead?

I ran until I felt safe. Then I realized I didn't know where Dad was. I was scared and alone.

I shouted for Dad for a long time,
and for a long time, I didn't find him.

Suddenly, one of the very
tall people knelt down.
Their face was full of worry,
and they were holding a big sign.

They asked if I needed help,
and I told them what had happened.

They let me sit on their shoulders,
so I could see over the forest of people.

They kept me safe while we searched and shouted. But we couldn't find Dad.

Until suddenly, I heard my name! Then I saw him! I jumped
down from my person-perch and ran to give Dad a big hug.

We stayed at the protest for a while. This time I held his hand tighter and yelled with the crowd, "No justice, no peace!"

We got home just before the sun went down, and after dinner I went straight to bed.

I wasn't really sleepy. It had been a sad and scary day.
But Dad said, "It'll be okay. I'll keep you safe, just like you kept your
butterfly safe. The sun will rise in the morning, like always."

And it did!

In the morning, I ate most of my toast before running
out the door. I fed my pets their favorite snacks.

And after a few days, my colorful monarch was all better!

I set it free outside and watched it fly
far away from anyone who would hurt it.

AUTHOR'S NOTE

When I was young, my mother and I lived in eastern Texas. We enjoyed our lives there, feeding our neighbor's horses, eating wild blackberries, and living surrounded by nature. Until James Byrd Jr. was murdered by a hate group near our home on June 7, 1998. My mother moved us across the country in hopes that I would live a full, happy life. We wound up in Saint Paul, Minnesota, where I found the arts and went to much more diverse schools. But I also grew to see that cruelty toward Black people was not just a southern issue.

Beginning in elementary school, I was treated differently in classes due to the color of my skin. In high school, I watched resource officers use unneeded force on Black teens regularly. As an adult I, along with many other Black people, have experienced countless traumas as Black folks around the nation are murdered by police.

The Minneapolis-Saint Paul metro area is one of the most unequal cities in the nation in terms of wealth, education, and police violence. Today, the median Black family in the Twin Cities area earns $38,178 a year—which is less than half of the median white family income of $84,459 a year. Also, the incarceration rate of Black people in the Twin Cities is eleven times that of white people, despite Black people only making up roughly one fifth of the population.

The Twin Cities has lost many Black lives at the hands of police. While only 20 percent of Minneapolis's population is Black, roughly 60 percent of police-reported uses of force target Black people, the most high-profile of these cases being Jamar Clark (murdered November 15, 2015), Philando Castile (murdered July 6, 2016), George Floyd (murdered May 25, 2020), and Winston Smith (murdered June 3, 2021). When George Floyd was murdered by Minneapolis police, our city and our nation had finally had enough. Minneapolis's Black folks and their allies demanded justice—but those demands were met with more violence at the hands of police and hate groups. During the racial uprising, it became clearer than ever that the police were more interested in protecting property (and white supremacy) than they were Black lives.

What kept many people going each night was the promise of the sun rising in the morning and the support of the community.

Minneapolis came together in a way I had never seen. Strangers became neighbors, neighbors became friends, and plans were made to protect as many people and homes as possible. Without the police to count on, a city came together to keep one another safe. It is more important than ever to take care of each other and speak out against injustice—in our homes, schools, neighborhoods, states, and nation. When we cannot trust the police to protect us, we must keep each other safe.

YOU CAN HELP

There are many ways to create change in your communities, from small acts of kindness to big gestures of solidarity.

YOU CAN DO THINGS LIKE THESE:

- Speak up for classmates who are being bullied (for their race, their gender, or any reason).

- Have difficult conversations at home about race.

- Read books by BIPOC (Black, Indigenous, and people of color) writers and books about their experiences.

- Ask your teachers difficult questions about race and history.

- Encourage friends and family to treat BIPOC individuals with kindness and respect.

- Make friends with people who are different from you.

- Make posters about racial equality.

- And above all else, be ready to learn! Keep an open mind about race issues and the hardships that other people experience.

DISCUSSION GUIDE FOR PARENTS AND EDUCATORS

Talking to kids about race, racism, and violence in policing can seem daunting. Kids of any age can start learning about this difficult reality. It's okay if you don't have all the answers. You can be a safe person for kids to talk to about this topic just by listening and caring.

Here are a few prompts and tips to guide your discussion:

TALK ABOUT THE STORY

Ask: How did this story make you feel?

Ask: What questions do you have about this story?

Ask: How did people help each other in this story?

DO POLICE HELP OR HURT?

In this story, Sarah's dad says that the police are supposed to "serve and protect us, but they hurt us instead." Police officers work in partnership with communities to uphold public safety, peace, and justice. They fight against crime and help to keep people safe.

People have been hurt as a result of police misconduct, abuse, and racial bias. Nearly 1,000 people are killed every year due to police-involved deadly use of force (specifically, shootings). People of color experience this violence more often. Black men are 2.5 times more likely to be killed by the police than white men.

The Say Her Name movement shed light on the untold stories of Black women who have been killed by the police, like Breonna Taylor.

WHY DO PEOPLE PROTEST?

Protesting is an act of standing up for what you believe in. People lift their voices for justice by peacefully marching, singing freedom songs, and holding up their fists together in solidarity. Protesting is just one method of nonviolent resistance. Other methods include boycotting, sit-ins, and mass petitions.

Protest is also a way to challenge a system and create change. During the Silent March of 1917, nearly 10,000 Black Americans marched in Harlem. Children and women dressed in white marched. They wore white to symbolize the innocence of the Black community killed in East Saint Louis as a result of racial terrorism. They marched in silence holding signs that read "Make America Safe for Democracy" and "Thou Shalt Not Kill." This was one of the first mass protests in US history.

CONTINUE THE CONVERSATION

Talking about racism and police violence with kids is not a one-time conversation. If you need more resources, connect with an educator, librarian, or local activist with experience in talking about racial injustice with kids. Just like in this story, there's a community of people around you ready to help.

DR. ARTIKA R. TYNER (A.K.A. MISS FREEDOM FIGHTER, ESQUIRE) is a passionate educator, an award-winning author, a civil rights attorney, a sought-after speaker, and an advocate for justice who is committed to helping children discover their leadership potential and serve as change agents in the global community. She is the founder of the Planting People Growing Justice Leadership Institute.